Bella's Birthday Unicorn

Don't miss any of Bella
and Glimmer's adventures!

Unicorn Magic

BOOK 2: Where's Glimmer?

Unicorn Magic

- Book 1 -
Bella's Birthday Unicorn

By Jessica Burkhart

Illustrated by Victoria Ying

Aladdin

New York London Toronto Sydney New Delhi

This book is a work of fiction. Any references to historical events, real people,
or real places are used fictitiously. Other names, characters, places, and events
are products of the author's imagination, and any resemblance to actual
events or places or persons, living or dead, is entirely coincidental.

ALADDIN

An imprint of Simon & Schuster Children's Publishing Division
1230 Avenue of the Americas, New York, NY 10020
This Aladdin paperback edition August 2014
Text copyright © 2014 by Jessica Burkhart
Cover illustrations copyright © 2014 by Victoria Ying
Interior illustrations by Victoria Ying
All rights reserved, including the right of reproduction in whole or in part in any form.
ALADDIN is a trademark of Simon & Schuster, Inc., and related logo
is a registered trademark of Simon & Schuster, Inc.
Also available in an Aladdin hardcover edition.
For information about special discounts for bulk purchases, please contact
Simon & Schuster Special Sales at 1-866-506-1949
or business@simonandschuster.com.
The Simon & Schuster Speakers Bureau can bring authors to your live event.
For more information or to book an event contact the
Simon & Schuster Speakers Bureau at 1-866-248-3049 or
visit our website at www.simonspeakers.com.
Cover designed by Jessica Handelman
Interior designed by Mike Rosamilia
The text of this book was set in Arno Pro.
Manufactured in the United States of America 0714 OFF
2 4 6 8 10 9 7 5 3 1
Library of Congress Control Number 2014936193
ISBN 978-1-4814-1105-9 (hc)
ISBN 978-1-4424-9822-8 (pbk)
ISBN 978-1-4424-9823-5 (eBook)

To Aly Heller,
for making magic with this series!

Acknowledgments

Thank you to everyone at Simon & Schuster for your enthusiasm over Unicorn Magic. Special thanks to Fiona Simpson, Bethany Buck, and Valerie Shea, and everyone on the sales team.

Victoria Ying, your illustrations couldn't be more perfect!

Also, thank you to Rubin Pfeffer and all my friends for your support.

Big shout-out to Team Canterwood! I hope you or a younger sibling enjoys this story.

Contents

1

Sleep? No Way!

"Bella! Time to get up for school!" Queen Katherine's voice came through the intercom system on Bella's wall.

From the window seat in her room, Princess Bella giggled at her mom's request. Little did Queen Katherine know that Bella had been up since the sun rose over the tall castle gates. In Bella's opinion, she had the best view of the castle grounds from her room in the North Tower. Early mornings were Bella's favorite time of day. She loved looking beyond the gates and over the Crystal Kingdom.

Bella got up, trotted to the intercom, and said, "Be down in a minute!"

She went back to her window seat, unable to tear herself away just yet. She looked at the lush green lawn and watched as the red roses, yellow daffodils, and purple lilies pushed up through the ground and opened into beautiful blooming flowers. Every night the flowers tucked themselves into their flower beds and slept under the giant moon. If Bella woke early enough, she could watch the flowers awaken, seemingly yawning and stretching as they reached for the sun.

A giant silver fish leaped out of the moat that surrounded the castle. The fish's fins glittered like a rainbow as it snapped at a dragonfly zooming over the water. The Protection Fish kept any unwanted intruders out of the water and helped the castle's royal guards. The fish were spelled to appear as menacing sharks to anyone who was not supposed to be on castle grounds.

The guards watched over the majestic grounds with fierce wolves. The wolves—almost twice the size of common gray wolves—had incredible senses. If a fierce wolf sensed danger, it would make eye contact with its prey. One gaze from a fierce wolf could hold an intruder in place. This gave a guard time to capture the paralyzed target.

In the center of the cobblestone driveway, the fountain flowed with clear water over the family crest sculpture. Thanks to a special shimmering spell, the water glistened as if it was filled with diamonds.

Toward the stables, the pastures were full of regal unicorns frolicking in the warm spring sun. Bella could watch the gorgeous creatures all day! She spotted two unicorns grazing together—one with its white coat, mane, and tail shaded green and the other tinted yellow. Kiwi and Scorpio. Her parents' unicorns. They stood out among the sea of white animals—only royal unicorns changed colors. The rest remained a dazzling white.

Unicorns were precious to Crystal and its neighboring kingdoms such as Menon, which related to the moon, and Foris, a kingdom filled with forests. In Crystal and the other kingdoms, a princess's or prince's eighth birthday was the most important birthday of all. The special celebration was a birthright that separated a royal from the regular townspeople.

Royals were born with an *aura*. King Phillip, Bella's father, had explained that an aura was a hazy light that glowed around a royal's body. Auras only showed themselves during a royal's eighth birthday and when a royal was being crowned king or queen.

Auras came in every color of the rainbow. One color, however, was one that *no one* wanted. Red auras meant the royal was dangerous. Evil. Even worse, a royal with a red aura wouldn't get the one special thing available only on his or her eighth birthday—a unicorn. It was tradition that royals were gifted with unicorns. If a royal did not get one, it left them not only without a best friend but also without a lifelong guardian.

Both of Bella's parents had amazing unicorns. Kiwi had been by Queen Katherine's side ever since her eighth birthday. Photos of baby Bella on Kiwi's back rested on the fireplace mantel in the main sitting room. Kiwi's best unicorn friend was Scorpio, King Phillip's lemon-shaded unicorn.

Bella headed to her canopy bed and straightened the lavender sheets and fluffy comforter. Lavender was one of her favorite colors. Sky blue—like her nightgown and slippers—was another. The colors made Bella happy even when she was in a bad mood.

She fixed her pillows on her bed and stepped

back to admire her handiwork. Even though she was a princess, Queen Katherine and King Phillip insisted that Bella make her bed. She didn't mind. Her two best friends in the entire universe, Ivy and Clara, did chores too. Ivy and Clara weren't from royal families, and Bella wanted to be as normal as her friends.

Ivy's father was one of the groundskeepers at Crystal Castle. Bella had met Ivy one day in one of the gardens—Violette Garden—when they were both six. The two had become instant friends. Bella had asked Ivy to bring any of her friends over to the castle whenever she liked. Ivy brought Clara over to the castle days later, and the three girls were soon best friends.

"This is *it*," Princess Bella whispered aloud. "My last morning as a seven-year-old."

She hurried over to her floor-length mirror and grabbed a brush off her nightstand. She ran it through her light-brown hair, so long it was down to the middle of her back.

Before Queen Katherine could call her again, Bella trotted out of her bedroom and darted down a staircase and into one of the castle's many hallways. Her slippers were silent over the stone floors as she hurried toward the dining room. It was a family joke that Bella had gotten lost in the castle every day until she'd turned six. Forty-two rooms and a dozen hallways would confuse anyone!

Bella sniffed the air, catching scents of her favorite breakfast foods like eggs and waffles. That made her hurry even faster! She got to the dining room, and Queen Katherine and King Phillip were already seated at the head of the table.

"Good morning, Bella!" King Phillip said. Bella's dad greeted her with a smile. "How did my favorite girl sleep?"

Bella slid into a velvet-cushioned high-backed

chair at the giant mahogany table. "Daaad!" she said. "Did *you* sleep at all when you were *this close* to your eighth birthday?"

Bella's father chuckled.

"So, I'm guessing you've been thinking a little about tomorrow?" King Phillip asked. He shared Bella's green eyes and brown hair. They both had pale skin. Bella had her mother's petite build. This morning, Queen Katherine's long, dark blond hair was in a loose braid down her back.

"A *little*? Um, only if 'a little' means every second of the day for, like, a week!" Bella answered. She felt like jumping out of her seat. "Turning eight is the most important day in my entire life! I can't wait!"

"Oh, Bells," her mom said. "It's a day that your father and I have been looking forward to celebrating with you since you were a baby."

"Tell me everything about Crystal's history," Bella said. "I want to hear it again."

"But we only just told you the very same thing *yesterday* morning!" Bella's father laughed.

"And the morning before that," her mother said.

The king, queen, and princess sat back as Thomas, one of the kitchen staff, pushed open the double doors from the kitchen and placed a plate in front of each of them.

"Thank you, Thomas," Bella said. "This looks delicious."

"You're welcome, Princess Bella," Thomas said, bowing his head.

Bella dug her fork into the scrambled eggs and eyed her waffle covered in strawberries and blueberries. With a mouthful of eggs, she stared at King Phillip with puppy eyes. "Pleeease," she said. "I promise, Dad—just one more time!"

Her dad put down his fork, smiling. "All right, Bella. I'll tell you the story one more time."

Bella clapped. "Yay!"

"A *very* long time ago, your great-great-great-great-grandfather King Scott, on your mother's side of the family, discovered a tiny piece of land," the king began. "To get there, he had crossed river rapids, survived dark forests, and scaled tall mountains. Finally he found himself standing amid a deserted space—a perfect spot right in the middle of a bunch of clouds! Now, King Scott had never stood among the clouds before. In fact, no one had! He was surprised to find the land was lush and plentiful. The grass there was the greenest he'd ever seen, the towering trees the tallest, and the fresh river that surrounded the land was the cleanest—it sparkled like a thousand diamonds in the moonlight."

"What about the sun?" Bella interrupted.

Her father winked. "The sun was perhaps the most important of all. The legend goes that the warmth of the sun, on the warmest and most beautiful morning where King Scott stood that following day, is what made unicorns from all the sky islands come to Crystal."

Bella could practically feel the sun's warmth on her cheeks when she closed her eyes and pictured the map of the four sky islands that hung in her classroom. They were giant pieces of land that floated high in the clouds and were only reachable from other islands when either a rainbow or moonbow spell was cast. Then the person who cast the spell could walk on the rainbow or moonbow to the other island.

Bella had traveled by rainbow once before. Never by moonbow. Walking on a rainbow felt a lot like walking up and then down escalator stairs.

Bella pictured the moonbows in her head. She had seen photos of them in her textbooks. Moonbows were just like rainbows except they flowed out of the moon and lit up the night sky with color.

"The beauty and magic of the sky," King Phillip

continued, "is why King Scott named our kingdom Crystal."

"You know the story by heart from here, Bells," King Phillip said. "King Scott encouraged his friends and their families to move to Crystal. They built houses, began families, and soon it was time to crown a king. Everyone in the kingdom wanted your great-great-great-great grandfather Scott to reign over all the people, since he'd discovered the kingdom."

"Then he was crowned king and our castle was built," Bella said. She put a forkful of tasty eggs into her mouth.

"Right," King Phillip said. "Your grandparents grew up here, and so did your mom. I lived in River Falls—a kingdom bordering Crystal."

Bella knew River Falls was on the same sky island as Crystal. There were so many kingdoms on each island that she couldn't name them all!

"Mom, you weren't much older than me when

Gram made *you* queen," Bella said. She took a bite of waffle.

Queen Katherine laughed. "I was *quite* a bit older than you. Your gram stepped down from the throne and passed her crown to me. That was around the time I met your dad."

Bella rolled her eyes as her parents made googly eyes at each other. *Ew!*

"What was it like when you were Paired to Kiwi and Scorpio?" Bella asked her parents.

A slight frown appeared, then was quickly covered by a smile on Queen Katherine's face. "Being Paired to Kiwi was one of the best moments in my life. When his aura turned green, I squealed so loud that I scared him!"

Bella giggled. "Dad?"

"I didn't squeal," King Phillip said. "But I was extremely excited to have a unicorn. Scorpio wouldn't let any of my friends ride him until I told him it was okay. He's still a very loyal unicorn."

The large clock in the foyer chimed nine a.m.

"I think it's time for you to get ready for school," Queen Katherine said. "Ivy and Clara will be here soon. Ms. Barnes is already preparing your lessons in the schoolroom."

Ivy and Clara had been attending the local school, but when the king and queen had seen how much Bella loved being around the two girls, they had invited Ivy and Clara to attend school at the castle along with a few other kids Bella's age. Bella had been homeschooled by a tutor since kindergarten, and now she couldn't imagine not having friends in her class.

Bella pushed back her chair and started toward her room. Footsteps quickly followed her.

"Good morning, Princess Bella."

"Hi, Lyssa," Bella said, stopping and smiling.

Lyssa was Bella's companion and handmaiden. She was a few years older than Bella—fourteen—and it was her job to help Bella get dressed and do homework, and make sure she had whatever else she needed. Lyssa had been by Bella's side for more than a year, and Bella loved her like an older sister.

"Let's get you dressed, shall we?" Lyssa asked. Together they walked to Bella's room.

"Something cheerful," Bella said. "You always know how to match the right clothes, Lyssa."

The blond girl smiled, tucking her long hair behind her ears. She wore a black skirt, ballet flats, and a collared light-pink shirt. Lyssa was one of the few employees at the castle who didn't have to wear a black uniform bearing Crystal's seal. Lyssa had told Bella that it was because Queen Katherine wanted Bella to forget that Lyssa was a member of the staff. Bella was glad, because the seal was *definitely* something that wasn't easy to ignore.

The Crystal seal was a giant diamond with two unicorns below. The rearing unicorns faced each other, and they stood on a scroll that read CRYSTAL KINGDOM.

Bella flipped on her closet lights and walked inside. The walls were bubblegum pink, with a coat of glitter paint that sparkled from the overhead chandelier and spotlights. Bella's clothes, on rotating racks, spun slowly so Bella and Lyssa could choose an outfit.

"Hmmm," Lyssa said, putting a finger to her lips. "How about . . ." She plucked a light-blue dress with white hearts from a rack and held it up for Bella's inspection.

"Yes, definitely!" Bella exclaimed. "And silver ballet flats? Would those match?"

Lyssa walked to the shoe racks, nodding. "Silver is perfect, Bella." Lyssa found the right shoes while Bella slipped out of her pj's and into the dress.

As she dressed, Bella couldn't stop thinking about what her father had said about his friends riding Scorpio. Bella wanted her unicorn to be loyal and love her, but she also wanted to give Ivy and Clara rides. Her nonroyal friends wouldn't get unicorns on their eighth birthdays. *I don't want them to think the unicorn is all mine and I'm never going to share,* Bella thought. That is, if she was actually Paired with a unicorn. The thought made her shudder. She'd never heard of a royal *not* getting a unicorn, but what if, for some crazy reason, she was the first?

"You're awfully quiet," Lyssa remarked. The older girl had pulled out a chair in front of Bella's mirror and held a hair brush.

Bella sat down, and Lyssa began brushing her hair.

"I'm just thinking about tomorrow," Bella said. "There's so much happening—the parade, the after-party, the Pairing Ceremony . . ."

"It's a lot," Lyssa said, nodding. "But remember that you've done big days like this your entire life. They've always been for your parents or grandparents, but tomorrow is *your* day. Celebrate—don't worry!"

Bella turned in her chair, reaching her arms up to hug Lyssa. "Thanks, Lys," she said. "You always make me feel better."

"What kind of help would I be if I didn't?" Lyssa asked with a grin.

"Bad help!" Bella teased back.

Lyssa put her hand over her heart. "That hurt, Bella," she said, pretending to be serious.

Bella, playing along, shrugged. "You always tell me to be honest. I mean, what if I didn't tell you that purple dress you had on last week was on backward?"

Lyssa's mouth dropped open. "Are you serious? Oh *no*! I can't believe it! I knew something was wrong—"

Bella turned around and grabbed Lyssa's hands. "Lys! I was kidding! I'm sorry! That dress was perfect *and* on the right way. I only brought it up because it was so cool that I wanted to borrow it one day."

Lyssa blew out a giant breath. "You scared me!" Laughing, she wrapped her arms around Bella. "Now I have to think about letting you wear it." She winked at Bella.

Lyssa left, headed for the classroom with Bella's schoolbooks. *I don't know how I'm going to concentrate on school today!* Bella thought.

When she heard the familiar chime of the doorbell, Bella realized that the answer to her question was easy! *And* standing right outside the front door to her castle.

Ivy and Clara, her two besties in the whole wide world, would be on Distraction Duty, starting now!

2

BFFs to the Rescue

"One day before you're older than Ivy and me!" Clara declared. She was the tallest of the three, and her long blond waves bounced as she hopped on tiptoes. Clara was the most outgoing and fearless of the group. In fact, Bella would never have even *met* Clara (even though Ivy had brought her to the castle) if Clara hadn't been brave enough to walk right up to Bella and say, "I know you! You're the princess! Is it fun being a princess?"

None of the other kids in Crystal had ever come up to Bella to talk to her the way Clara did. Bella admired how fearless Clara could be—she often wished she could feel even half as brave as her friend.

Now, all three girls walked down the castle hallway to the sunny room where their lessons were held every weekday. Six other kids of castle employees attended school in the royal classroom.

"You're so lucky," Ivy said. She tucked a lock of straight, chin-length blond hair behind her ear. "I can't wait to turn eight!" Ivy was the opposite of Clara—she was quieter and listened more. That meant Ivy always had the best gossip!

Bella nodded. "I wonder if I'll feel any different tomorrow."

"I bet you'll wake up at exactly midnight," Clara said. "Or maybe you won't be able to sleep at all! You're going to be Paired tomorrow!"

Paired.

The thought alone made Bella's stomach do backflips *and* rumble nervously at the same time.

"Do you think Troy will bring a toad to class again today?" Bella asked, quickly changing the subject.

Clara wrinkled her nose. "He better not, or I'll toss him in the moat!"

Laughing, Bella felt relieved. Her attempt to stop all Bella's Birthday Talk had worked.

Ivy rifled through the pages of her red notebook. "I wanted to show you guys a sketch that I made of the royal unicorns," she said. "But it's invisible now. Ms. Barnes must have activated the invisible ink spell until after our spelling quiz."

Ivy held up her notebook, its pages blank. Ms. Barnes often used invisible ink spells on test or quiz days so no one could cheat by looking at his or her notes. But she made sure that the spell only lasted until the exams were turned in. After, everyone's notes returned to normal.

"Definitely show it to us after," Bella said.

The school bell sounded from inside the classroom. Time to go!

The girls hurried inside the classroom and took their usual seats in the front row.

"Good morning, everyone," Ms. Barnes said. "As you may have noticed, all of your notebooks are blank and will be until we've finished our spelling quiz. I hope you studied last night."

A small groan came from the back of the room. Bella didn't have to turn around to know it was her friend Evan. He never studied and was always being asked to stay after class.

"Take out a fresh sheet of paper and a pencil," Ms. Barnes said from the front of the classroom. "We'll begin."

Ivy, Bella, and Clara didn't have a free second to talk the rest of the morning. Bella counted down the seconds until lunch period.

* * *

"Ah! I thought we would never get to talk ever again!" Clara said.

The three friends had grabbed their favorite table on one of the castle's back decks. A cheery orange umbrella stuck up from the middle of the table and shielded the girls from the sun.

Along with their turkey sandwiches and different side dishes, each girl had extra helpings of Crystal's famous "sunray pie." Bella didn't know exactly how the pie was made, but she did know that it contained sunray berries. Sunray berries grew on vines that stretched into the clouds and out of sight. The people of Crystal said the vines were connected to the sun.

When farmers picked the berries, they had to wear extra-dark sunglasses because the berries were so bright! They glowed sunny yellow, and inside the piecrust were circles shaped like the sun that made Bella feel happy the second she took a bite. The pie tasted sweet—from the sun-ray berries—and refreshing, like lemonade, at the same time.

"I was trying not watch the clock, but I kept looking at it!" Ivy added.

Bella knew her friends wanted to talk about tomorrow—her birthday—but it was the last thing she wanted to bring up. This was the first time Bella noticed how very different *her* life was from her friends'.

Bella didn't feel lonely with kids her own age at the castle. But now she realized she would be on her own at her Pairing Ceremony—the biggest event in her life so far!

"Guess what? My dad said he's taking me to River Falls one day," Bella continued. She wasn't exactly lying to her friends—her dad had said that. But it was weeks ago, and she'd forgotten about it until now. "Dad wants to show me where he was born. I heard there are Fall Frogs that are as big as cats!"

"Whoa!" Ivy said. "That will be a fun trip! But I just learned about something way creepier than frogs. My sister's friend told us that these spiders called Anasi live deep the Crystal woods. They're prankster spiders—they appear to shift into whatever the person who's nearby is imagining."

"They can turn into *people*?" Bella asked, shuddering. "A spider-person! Ewww!"

Ivy and Clara made yeah-totally-gross faces too.

"But the spiders just create a vision—they don't really become something else," Ivy continued. "When the person gets close enough, the spider stops the trick and scares the person by showing itself as a spider."

"I can't think about creepy spiders anymore!" Bella said. Her skin felt crawly. "I'm so glad I've never seen one."

"I heard something too," Clara said. She clearly didn't want to be the only one who didn't have something to add about a new creature.

"One night I couldn't sleep, so I started to go downstairs for milk," Clara said. "My parents were talking and I stopped and listened."

"Eavesdropper!" Bella said, teasing.

"I couldn't help it!" Clara said. "It was too interesting. I heard my parents talking about an old lady who lives on the edge of town. She only comes out during big royal celebrations. They said she's so jealous that red smoke poofs around her. She travels with this band of, like, bad unicorns."

"Bad unicorns?" Ivy asked.

"Unicorns that probably bite your fingers off," Clara said.

With that, the girls all burst into giggles over their silly, scary stories of creatures and old ladies.

Lunch period was minutes from ending, and Bella sighed quietly with relief. She had managed to avoid talking about her birthday. She picked up her empty tray—even the tiniest crumb of sunray pie gone—and started to stand.

"Oh, Bells!" Ivy said. "What time should Clara and I come over tomorrow? I'm *so* excited!"

Bella stood slowly. "Six," she said, her tone a little uncertain.

Clara and Ivy nodded.

"Wow, your birthday starts early!" Clara said. "But I'll be up on time and at the castle by six a.m."

Oh no, Bella thought. Now she had to tell Ivy and Clara something awful.

"I actually meant six in the evening," Bella said. She paused, looking at her tray for a second. "I have the royal parade and press stuff to do before I get home for my party."

"Ha, ha," Ivy said, grinning. "You're joking,

Bella. What time do you *really* want us to come over?"

Bella wanted to cry. Sometimes being a princess was no fun at all!

"I'm so, so sorry," Bella said. "I've been *begging* my mom to make an exception this year so you can both be in the parade with me. But she won't budge. She keeps saying it's 'royal tradition' and we have to follow the rules."

Ivy and Clara sat unmoving. They both had huge frowns on their faces.

"That's such an old tradition!" Clara said. "We're your *best* friends! Your mom won't let us be in the parade at all?"

"We're not *royal*, Clara," Ivy snapped. "Don't forget that Bella is a princess. There are things that you and I—just regular people—can't do. I guess being with our best friend on her birthday is one of them."

Tears pricked Bella's eyes. The sunray pie swirled in her stomach.

"You guys have no idea how hard I've been fighting to change the rules," Bella pleaded with Ivy and Clara. "I agree—it's a silly tradition! I've been begging my mom every single day. I want you two there for every minute of my birthday. Especially this one."

Clara stood, not looking at Bella, and picked up her tray. "Don't waste your time, Princess. In fact, forget about coming to *my* eighth birthday party."

Ivy nodded, standing next to Clara. "Mine too. I don't want any royals at my party."

Ivy and Clara, trays in hand, hurried away from the table, leaving Bella in tears.

3

Princess Confessions

Later that afternoon, Bella flopped onto her stomach on her bed. She actually wished her teacher had assigned homework—she needed something, *anything*, to keep her mind from racing ahead to tomorrow. *And to stop me from thinking about how mad Ivy and Clara are at me,* Bella thought.

She changed into comfy after-school clothes—bright yellow leggings and a plain white T-shirt—then left her room to wander the castle's hallways. When Queen Katherine had taken the throne, she had completely redecorated. Bella's mom had told her daughter that she wanted the castle to feel "welcoming."

New rugs, all a warm, cherry-red color, covered much of the hallway floors. Beautiful wrought-iron candelabras lit by long ivory taper candles hung along the walls every few feet, illuminating the lovely artwork decorating the castle's royal walls. Even the dusty, old, heavy drapes that had hung over the large palace windows had been replaced by the queen with light, airy curtains.

Bella hurried up two flights of stairs to the main tower. She skidded to a stop in front of her parents' open bedroom door. Queen Katherine tilted her head toward the door where her daughter stood. She put the pile of mail in her hand down on her bedside table and smiled at her daughter. Queen Katherine waved Bella into the bedroom.

"I've never seen anyone move so slowly," her mom joked. Then she saw the look on Bella's face. "What's wrong, Bells?"

Bella crossed the room and sank into the cushy

white-and-blue comforter. It felt like she was sitting on pillows. She traced an index finger over one of the swirly designs.

She shrugged, not looking up. "Nothing. Okay, something. But it's silly."

"I love hearing about silly things," Queen Katherine replied. "Especially from you."

Bella looked up into her mom's hazel eyes and took a giant breath. "I'm scared about tomorrow," she began.

Queen Katherine put a hand on her daughter's knee but stayed silent.

"I'm nervous about the parade," Bella continued. "What if no one comes? I'll be *so* embarrassed—plus, it'll be upsetting to you and Daddy."

"Is that all?" the queen asked. "Are you sure there's nothing else bothering you?"

Bella frowned. Her mom knew her way too

well. *I won't get away with keeping anything from Mom,* she thought.

"I'm scared that I won't be Paired with a unicorn. What if one just doesn't exist for me?" Bella asked.

Queen Katherine tilted her head, smiling at Bella. "Sweetie, I have no doubt that a *very* special unicorn is waiting for you. He or she is probably in the royal stables right now, thinking, 'When am I going to meet Princess Bella?'"

Bella giggled. "You really think so?"

"I know so," Queen Katherine answered. "I want you to tell me these things, Bells. Whatever you're worried about—big or small—so that tomorrow will be as amazing for you as possible."

Bella chewed on the inside of her cheek. "There is one more thing. I feel bad having all of this attention on me, tomorrow, when Ivy and Clara will never have a birthday like mine," she said. "We got in a fight today because I had to tell them they couldn't be in the parade with me. What if they get so jealous that they decide to stop being my friends? There is so much about this birthday that they'll never have. I mean, getting a unicorn is such a *big* deal!"

Queen Katherine took her hand from Bella's knee and ran it over Bella's hair. The familiar gesture soothed Bella a little.

"Tomorrow is a huge day for you, Bells," Queen Katherine said. "But Ivy and Clara have never been jealous that you're a princess. They became your best friends knowing exactly who you are."

"I know, but they don't get to participate in anything tomorrow," Bella said. "They have to watch me in the parade, and they can't even come to the Pairing Ceremony because it's only for royals. They're *really* upset."

"They'll still be at your party after the parade," Bella's mom pointed out.

"But they're so mad," Bella said. "I don't even think they're coming to my party."

She buried her face into a pillow on her mom's bed. The queen wasn't going to budge, Clara and Ivy were going to stay mad at her, and tomorrow wasn't going to be half as special without her friends.

4

Happy Birthday!

Princess Bella was wide awake even before her rainbow-shaped alarm clock went off. Sometimes she liked to set her alarm instead of her mom waking her up.

Shortly after, there was a knock at her door, and Queen Katherine and King Phillip stepped inside Bella's bedroom.

"Happy birthday, Bella!" Queen Katherine, clad in a plush white robe, exclaimed. She hurried to Bella's bedside and kissed her forehead.

"Happy eighth birthday, sweetheart," said King Phillip. He ruffled Bella's hair after kissing her cheek.

"I can't believe it!" Bella said excitedly. "I'm *eight*! I thought I'd be up all night and counting down until midnight, but I fell asleep."

Her parents laughed.

"Throw on a robe and come to the breakfast table," Queen Katherine said. "Your favorite breakfast is ready."

Once her parents left Bella's room, she flopped back onto her pillow. *I'm eight! I'm eight!* she chanted over and over in her head. She had been dreaming about this day for as long as she could remember. It was time to get her birthday started! Then Bella remembered. Ivy and Clara. She had called them last night, but neither of her friends had answered.

You have to at least smile and pretend to be happy for Mom and Dad, Bella thought.

She put her feet into fuzzy pink slippers and pulled her terry-cloth robe over her matching shorts and T-shirt pj's. She dashed to the breakfast table. All of the castle staff—the chefs, gardener, stable workers, Lyssa, maids—had gathered around the table. They smiled and chanted, "Happy birthday, Princess Bella!"

Bella blushed as pink as her slippers. "Thank you," she said to everyone.

Color-changing streamers that twirled in the air hung from the ceiling and formed a canopy around the breakfast table. Glittery balloons flashed on and off as they floated from the floor to the ceiling and back down again.

Plates, ready to be filled, hovered at the start of a luxurious breakfast buffet. Fruit, waffles, eggs, bacon, and sausage filled silver trays. A glass filled itself with orange juice for Bella, and two mugs soon were brimming with coffee for her parents. Bella's plate, waiting in front of her, moved toward the buffet—ready to fill itself with whatever food Bella wanted.

"Ooh, this is so beautiful!" Bella said happily, clapping her hands. "Can we start eating now?"

Everyone laughed. King Phillip pulled out a chair for Bella and she took her seat, ready to dive into her birthday breakfast. Bella gulped her entire glass of juice first.

Lyssa poured Bella another glass of OJ, and the pitcher refilled itself. Bella glanced at the waffles and her plate wafted through the air, stopping in front of the waffles.

"Two, please," Bella said.

Two steaming waffles lifted from the silver tray and slid onto Bella's plate. Immediately, new waffles replaced the ones that had floated to her plate.

She grinned and looked at the fruit. Her plate was going to get a workout today!

*　*　*

After a delicious start to her birthday, Bella trotted up the stairs to her room with Lyssa.

"I can't believe I'm finally going to see my birthday dress!" Bella said.

Lyssa smiled. "You're going to love it!"

Bella eyed Lyssa. "I can't believe I haven't been able to convince you to tell me *anything* about it. Mom hasn't spilled one detail."

"Close your eyes," Lyssa said, taking Bella's hand.

She felt as though soda bubbles were bursting in her stomach.

She shut her eyes tight and let Lyssa lead the way to her dress.

"Okay! Open!" Lyssa squeezed Bella's hand.

Bella's mouth dropped open.

"Oh my gosh, Lyssa! It's gorgeous!" she squealed.

The blush-colored dress was satin, covered with a delicate layer of lace. Holding her breath, Bella slowly walked up to the dress and touched the cap sleeves. A satin sash cinched the dress's waist. Gray ballet flats covered in iridescent sequins were on the floor under the dress. A delicate silver chain with a letter *B* hung on the hanger.

Bella spun in a circle to look at Lyssa. "This was *so* worth keeping a secret! It's the best dress ever!"

Lyssa grinned. "Seems like you kind of like it."

"Only a little bit," Bella joked. "Will you help me get dressed?"

As Lyssa started to help Bella, the princess felt a pang of sadness. Normally, Bella would be snapping photos of her dress and sending them to Ivy and Clara. She couldn't even stand the thought that her two best friends might never see her dress.

Lyssa helped Bella change from her pajamas

into her dress. Bella slid her feet into the ballet slippers while Lyssa clasped the necklace around her neck.

Unable to wait another second, Bella turned toward her full-length mirror.

"It's the prettiest dress ever!" Bella sighed happily.

She twirled in front of the mirror, loving how the layers of her dress spun out in front of her. Her mom and the seamstress had captured everything Bella could want in a dress. The shade of pink was Bella's favorite, and the fabric swished around her knees. *I really feel like a princess today!* Bella thought.

"Bella?" Queen Katherine called, knocking on Bella's door.

"Mom, come in!" Bella faced the door, grinning. Lyssa stood back and clasped her hands.

"Oh, Bella!" Queen Katherine put a hand over

her mouth. The other hand held an old wooden box. It was a deep polished mahogany with gold corners and a gold lock. "You look *beautiful*."

Bella hurried over and wrapped her arms around her mom. "Thanks, Mom. I love my dress so much."

"It's perfect for your big day," Queen Katherine said.

Bella started to ask what was inside the box when her mom asked, "Would you like me to do your hair?"

"Yes, please!" Bella said, checking her ruffled hair—definitely not parade worthy—in the mirror.

She sat at the purple-velvet-cushioned chair with gold that twisted into vines to make the chair's arms and legs. Her mom put the box on Bella's bed.

"Lyssa," Queen Katherine said. "Feel free to leave and get yourself ready for the parade."

"Thank you, Queen Katherine," Lyssa said. She

bowed her head to the queen and winked at Bella as she left the room.

Queen Katherine took a large brush and ran it through Bella's hair, gently combing out the tangles. Bella watched in the mirror, hoping she'd be able to copy the look one day, but Queen Katherine was too fast. Within minutes, the queen had swept Bella's hair into an elegant half-updo.

"What do you think?" Bella's mom asked.

"I love it, Mom!" Bella said, looking at her hair in the mirror. "Thank you so much!"

Bella started to get up, but her mom placed a hand on her shoulder. "There's one more thing I need to do to finish your look," Queen Katherine said.

"Oh, okay." Bella settled back into the chair.

Queen Katherine appeared by Bella's side with the mystery box in hand.

"I think this will add a little sparkle," the queen said.

Bella turned in her chair, peeking into the box. Queen Katherine opened the lid and inside, resting on a blue pillow, was a glittering tiara. Not just *any* tiara either. Bella had a princess tiara that she wore during royal events and celebrations. *This* tiara was clearly made for Bella's birthday.

Bella's mouth fell open "Wow," she breathed. "I get to wear this tiara? Are you serious?" She clutched her chest and couldn't stop herself from bouncing on her toes.

Queen Katherine laughed. "Very serious. Your father and I went into the jewel vault this morning and retrieved it. This tiara was made the day you were born, and we've kept it under lock and key until your eighth birthday."

Bella stared at the diamonds, which shone and winked at her. The tiara had intricate swirls and curls that formed a heart at the center. A teardrop-shaped diamond dangled from the middle of the heart.

Queen Katherine took the tiara from its pillow and carefully lowered it onto her daughter's head. Bella couldn't stop staring at it—it was the prettiest thing she had ever seen.

"Now," Queen Katherine said, meeting Bella's gaze in the mirror, "you are ready for the parade."

Bella stared at herself in the mirror, trying to keep up her smile, but her chin wobbled.

"Oh, sweetie," her mom said. "What is wrong?"

"Today would be perfect if Clara and Ivy were able to celebrate with me. I'm happy, Mom, but I'm sad they're angry with me."

Queen Katherine leaned close to Bella's ear. "I wasn't going to say a word, but . . ."

When the queen finished whispering in Bella's ear, Bella let out a loud squeal.

"Mom!" she said. "This is the most magical day of my whole life."

"I'm happy to hear it," Queen Katherine said,

smiling. "You deserve one day to have whatever you wish."

Bella squealed again and hugged her mom tight. Her birthday was off to a perfect start!

5

Parade Princess

After one last check to make sure everything looked perfect, Princess Bella had dashed out of the castle and into a special carriage that took her to the start of her official birthday celebration.

Queen Katherine, King Phillip, and Bella had taken the royal carriage they used only for special occasions. It was powered by Crystal's pride and joy—the sun itself! The royal carriage needed only a royal driver to steer. The carriage glowed like a giant orb. Usually, Bella stared out the clear exterior with her nose pressed against the glass as they made their way down the winding roads from the castle to town. This time, she'd sat silent with her hands clasped in her lap. She was nervous *and* excited.

The royal carriage stopped at the beginning of the parade route. Tons of people were already lined up behind the shield spell on either side of the cobblestone road.

"Your mom and I will see you at the end of the parade, Bells," King Phillip said. "Have fun!" Her mom kissed Bella's cheek. "We're heading to our float just in front of yours."

Bella stepped out of the royal carriage, and flashbulbs popped. Her parents exited the opposite side with royal security. They wanted all of the attention to be on Bella on her special day.

Crystal's weather seemed to know it was Bella's birthday—sunlight beamed down, there wasn't a cloud in the sky, and the temperature was unseasonably warm.

Just like her mom had taught her, Bella stopped and turned to wave at the newspaper and TV crews. A dozen or so men and women had notebooks, giant cameras and recorders, and microphones. It was a little scary, but Bella remembered the security guards at her sides and the shield spell.

The location calmed Bella too. The royal carriage had stopped at the edge of town in a grassy field filled with daisies and clusters of wild tulips. Bella loved the pops of color. It looked like pieces of a rainbow had been sprinkled in the field! The parade floats had lined up, and Crystal's police patrolled the area with fierce wolves. None of the wolves had teeth bared, so no danger was near.

Now Bella could really see the sparkly line of the shield spell along the sides of the parade route. The spell glittered—a sign it had been cast by a royal—so none of the townspeople could break the barrier. Only a royal could disarm the spell.

"Princess Bella! A photo for the *Daily Crystal*?" a man with a camera asked Bella with a smile.

"Sure!" Bella said. The security guards moved off to the sides, and Bella smiled at the camera.

More flashbulbs popped as other reporters crowded in to catch a shot of Bella. She stood for a moment to let everyone get a photograph. Bella jutted out a hip, putting her hand on her side, and grinned.

"Thank you, Princess," the reporter from the *Daily Crystal* said.

Bella nodded. "Of course! I hope you got a good picture!" She may have spent her life growing up as a royal, but her parents had always been fiercely protective of her in the media. Until today, most of the media coverage centered on her parents.

The reporters laughed. "It's your birthday," a woman said, adjusting the lens on her camera.

"Pictures always come out good on someone's birthday."

Bella looked at everyone, taking it all in. The *Daily Crystal* was on the breakfast table every morning, and usually the only royals in the paper were her parents. Now it was Bella's turn.

"A quick question, Princess?" the *Daily Crystal* reporter asked. He let his camera hang around his neck and pulled out a small notepad. "My name is Dan, by the way."

"Sure," Bella said. "Pleased to meet you, Dan."

Inside, she smiled. Her parents would be so proud of her manners if they were here.

"First, I would like to wish you a happy eighth birthday," Dan said. "Second, I would like to know, what is your favorite part of this birthday?"

Other reporters scrambled to get out their gadgets to catch Bella's answer. Many of them pressed the bridge of their frameless glasses, and with the blink of a blue light, the glasses started recording wherever the reporter looked.

"My favorite part is having no school," Bella said. "So that I can spend the day with my best friends and family!"

Someone tapped Bella on the shoulder, and she turned around. Bella grinned when she saw who they were.

"You guys are here!" she said happily.

Ivy and Clara had been escorted to Bella. The girls all hugged as cameras clicked and flashes went off, but Bella ignored the lights.

"Your dress!" Clara said, her blue-green eyes wide.

"It's so pretty!" Ivy added.

"Thank you! You both look like princesses!" Bella told her friends.

She said a silent thank-you to Queen Katherine. Only the queen would be able to get beautiful dresses for Bella's best friends *and* make sure the girls could accompany Bella on her royal float.

"Can we talk to you for a minute?" Ivy asked.

"Please," Clara added. "We know you're busy, but we have to talk to you."

Bella nodded and took Ivy and Clara by their elbows and led them away from the crowd. She pulled them into a clear tent—it had been concocted with a sunshield spell. They could see out of the walls, but no one could see in. The sunshield spell gave the people a break from the sun if they entered.

Ivy and Clara hung their heads.

"Bella," Ivy said. "Clara and I are *so* sorry for what we said to you at lunch."

Clara nodded. "Ivy and I know that you're a princess and it would be silly of us to think you could change a tradition that has been in place for hundreds of years."

"But you *did*," Ivy said. "Your mom called our moms and told them how you wouldn't have a good birthday without your best friends."

Bella blinked fast, holding back tears. "I couldn't imagine spending today with you two mad at me *and* not in the parade or coming to my party tonight."

"Ivy and I were awful to you," Clara admitted. "But you and your mom not only got invites for us to be in the parade, but your mom also got us these amazing dresses."

"My mom did the whole thing," Bella said. "She told me at the last minute that you two were coming and asked if I wanted to help choose your dresses. At first, I thought she was kidding! You both were so mad at me that I didn't think you'd even want to come to the parade."

"We acted like spoiled brats," Ivy said. "We always wanted to be with you on your birthday."

She smiled. "Especially in dresses like these!"

"Ivy," Bella said, "I chose that emerald dress just for you because I know it's your favorite color."

Ivy's mouth opened and closed.

Bella turned to Clara. "I picked plum for you because it's your favorite fruit. I wanted to have a rose on the neckline because you love roses so much."

"I love my dress," Ivy said softly. "And I'm so sorry."

"Me too," Clara said.

"Though I wouldn't blame you if you didn't like *either* of us right now," Ivy interjected.

Bella half smiled and shook her head. "That's silly. Of course I still like you both. You're my best friends."

"We didn't act like it," Ivy said. "This is your day, Bella, and I'm so sorry I did something to make it less special."

"I'm sorry, Bella," Clara said. "Really sorry—I'm glad one of my best friends is a princess. I'm okay that I'm not one. But like the type of friend you are, you found a way to make Ivy and me feel like princesses too."

Bella's friends lowered their eyes and stared at the stones beneath their feet. Even though she was still a little hurt, Bella didn't want them fighting, and she certainly didn't want anything to be off with the three of them for the rest of her birthday.

"Hugs, already!" Bella said. She opened her arms.

Clara and Ivy looked up at Bella, their eyes wide. Squealing, they almost knocked her over with a giant bear hug. They pulled apart and smiled at each other.

"I need bestie power right now," Bella said. "All I can think about is the Unicorn Pairing Ceremony."

"You've got it," Clara said. "But are you sure

that you still want us to come over?" She fidgeted with the front of her dress.

"Yes, are you sure?" Ivy asked. "Clara and I talked about it on the ride over. You know that we are a million percent happy for you, right? We know we're not princesses, but we're not jealous of you, Bella. We would *never* be. You're our BFF, and we really want to come to the castle and party with you!"

Tears filled Bella's eyes. She didn't want her nose to turn red, like it always did when she cried, but she couldn't stop a tear from falling.

"Bella! Don't cry!" Clara said. "Is something else wrong?"

"Nothing—everything is so perfect," Bella said. "I knew you guys wouldn't be jealous, but a tiny part of me was scared that you would be. I don't want to lose you as my best friends just because of this silly princess thing."

"Never!" Ivy and Clara said at the same time.

All three girls laughed.

"You're stuck with us," Clara said.

"Forever," Ivy added.

Giggling, the three girls hugged again.

6

Smile and Wave!

Bella smiled as she walked toward her float. Security, almost enough for a royal wedding, walked beside her. The fight with her friends had been a nightmare. Now, everything could be about including Ivy and Clara.

Bella spotted her float before the guards could point it out. The second float in line shimmered and glowed with lavender and sky-blue lights and flowers. Light-blue fog settled above the float and sheer purple fog stretched around the bottom. Four tall posts, mimicking a canopy bed, had light-purple tulle draped from each of them and across the top of the float. At the front, lights in cursive script blinked HAPPY BIRTHDAY, PRINCESS!

An oversize throne in the middle of the float was just the right size to fit Bella, Ivy, and Clara. Bella knew from past parades that the floats were all preprogrammed to follow the parade route.

"Princess, please allow me to help you and your friends aboard," one of the guards said.

In no time Bella, Clara, and Ivy stood on the float. The girls grinned at each other. They had been instructed to keep a hand on the railing unless they were seated. Bella stood at the front of the float and Ivy and Clara were on opposite sides, practicing their parade waves. Bella had never seen bigger smiles on her friends' faces.

"It's time!" a man with a bullhorn called from atop a prancing unicorn. "People of Crystal, please join me in wishing Princess Bella a happy birthday! Let the parade begin!"

Queen Katherine and King Phillip's float lifted a few inches above the ground, hovering, and started forward. The king and queen stood at the front of their elegant red-and-gold float and began waving as soon as they reached the start of the crowd.

Here we go! Bella thought excitedly.

There was a crackle in the air and thousands of tiny lights—like fireflies—appeared at each corner of Bella's float. The lights whirled in circles and propelled the float forward. The cheers of the crowd grew louder and louder. Bella wondered if people in the next kingdom could hear the people chanting, "Happy birthday, Princess!" Nerves rumbled in Bella's stomach. *I can do this,* she told herself. *Just smile and wave! That's it!*

Ivy and Clara reached into the large buckets that hung beside them and grabbed handfuls of candy, including Sunstix—a stick of candy that

glowed in the dark and did the same to the person's tongue!

They tossed the treats into the crowd. Bella smiled as she watched little kids chase after the scattered candy. Watching them made her nerves evaporate. She dipped a hand into her own bucket and threw a bunch of sweets toward a group of young girls. The girls held a sign with glittery pink letters spelling WE ♥ PRINCESS BELLA! When they saw Bella had noticed the float, the girls released the sign, and the letters floated into the air before disappearing with a *poof* over the crowd and raining silver sparkles.

Behind the royal floats, royal soldiers led fierce wolves that performed tricks for the audience. All kinds of instruments floated down the parade route playing upbeat music. Bella couldn't see the performers, but she knew fire eaters, enchanted animals, and spell casters walked the route and entertained the crowd. Security guards walked beside the royal family. *This is a* lot *of security, even for a royal parade!* Bella thought. But the king and queen had always gone overboard on safety measures for Bella.

Bella's float wound along the parade route, and there wasn't one empty spot behind the shield spell. Princess Bella tossed as much candy as she could and waved and smiled for pictures. She looked behind her at Ivy and Clara. Both girls furiously tossed candy to keep up with the outstretched hands.

"This is so crazy!" Clara shouted to Bella.

"And ridiculously fun!" Ivy added.

"I'm so glad you're both here," Bella said.

"Happy birthday, Princess!" someone called from the crowd. A familiar voice.

She scanned the rows of people and saw Lyssa smiling and waving at her. Bella waved furiously at

Lyssa and almost hopped up and down at seeing her friend in the crowd.

She took a deep breath, wanting to remember the moment forever, and glanced up at the sky. And noticed something odd.

Bella blinked and shut her eyes, hoping when she opened them that what she had seen would be gone. But there it was—a giant, billowing plume of red smoke. The float turned a corner, and Bella realized where that smoke was coming from.

The Dark Forest.

7

Parade Panic

As soon as the crowd caught sight of the smoke, panic spread from person to person. People were pointing and shouting, Bella's celebration temporarily forgotten.

Any activity from the Dark Forest and the Blacklands was *not* good. Bella didn't know much about the Dark Forest or the Blacklands, but she did know one thing: *Never* go there. She had been taught since she could walk that the Blacklands and Dark Forest were dangerous and she was never to set foot on those grounds bordering Crystal. Bella had heard rumors about an evil queen ruling the lands, but her parents always said the same thing when she confronted them: "We'll tell you about it when you're older."

She really wanted to talk to her mom and dad, but they had their heads together on their float a few feet in front. The princess gripped the float's railing tightly, in shock that this was happening on her big day. Was that why there was extra security? Bella wondered.

"Your Majesty!"

"Is evil threatening Crystal? What shall we do?"

The townspeople shouted questions at the king and queen as they climbed down from their float.

"C'mon," Bella said. She grasped Ivy's and Clara's hands as a security guard helped them to the ground. "We have to find out what's going on."

The three girls hurried up to Bella's parents. "Mom?" Bella asked as she reached her mother's side. "What's going on?"

"Shhh, sweetie," Queen Katherine said. She placed a hand on her daughter's head. "Dad's going to address everyone. The smoke isn't anything to worry about."

"But—," Bella started, but she was interrupted by the crackle of a bullhorn.

Silently, Lyssa appeared at Bella's side. Since she worked at the castle, Lyssa was able to slip through the shield spell. Bella slipped her hand into the older girl's comforting grasp.

King Phillip, sword gleaming at his side, was atop the podium in the town's center.

"Kind people of Crystal," King Phillip said. Bella realized her dad was using his deep I'm-king-so-listen voice. She, Clara, and Ivy huddled together next to Queen Katherine.

"The smoke is merely a misguided birthday message to my daughter," King Phillip continued. "Neither you nor our fair kingdom is under attack.

As a precaution to ensure that everyone continues to enjoy this glorious day, extra guards will patrol Crystal's boundaries. Please go about your plans and do not let this act of childishness ruin the spirit of Princess Bella's birthday."

"Whew," Ivy said in a whisper. "Your dad doesn't seem worried, Bella."

"I was scared for a minute," Clara added.

"But who's sending the smoke signal?" Bella asked. "Why would it be a birthday message to me?"

She met her mother's eyes. Queen Katherine was worried. "I'm going to speak to your father," the queen said. "I'll be back in a moment."

Bella's mom was gone only moments, but it felt like hours before she returned.

"You two better say good-bye to your parents before you come to the castle for my party," Bella told her friends. She managed a smile despite her nerves.

Ivy and Clara nodded and started into the crowd. Since they were on the inside of the shield spell, they'd be able to cross over. Plus, it was time to drop the shield.

"Lyssa," Queen Katherine said as she arrived beside Bella, "please make sure the royal carriage is prepared for our ride home. Thank you."

"Yes, Your Majesty," Lyssa said, bowing her head. She squeezed Bella's hand before disappearing into the crowd.

"Mom?" Bella asked. "What's wrong? What was that?"

Queen Katherine lowered her hazel eyes to Bella. "It's nothing. Everything is okay."

"I can tell you're scared," Bella said, slipping her hand into her mom's. "Maybe we should cancel my party."

"Bella, listen to me," Queen Katherine said, leaning close to her daughter. "You mustn't worry.

Your father and I will protect you, the castle, and Crystal from anything bad. Today is your eighth birthday. Please let me do any worrying that needs to be done, and promise me you'll enjoy your party."

The queen squeezed Bella's hand. Bella watched the red smoke billow from the distance and couldn't help but cringe.

"Okay, Mom. I won't worry—promise."

Queen Katherine smiled and hugged Bella. "Good girl."

Bella hugged her mom and chewed the inside of her cheek, wondering if she could keep that promise.

8

What Red Smoke?

A couple of hours later, the weird red smoke was the *last* thing on Bella's mind. She was too full to think of anything but her stomach. Bella, Ivy, and Clara had feasted on delicious roast chicken, mac 'n' cheese, and all of Bella's favorite foods.

After dinner, the chefs brought out an eight-tiered cake—one layer for every year since Bella's birth. The gorgeous cake had been covered in light-purple buttercream frosting, and each layer was decorated with images of Bella's favorite things. Unicorns, flowers, and bumblebees floated in the air around the cake and looked real until you swiped a hand through them—and it became clear they were images projected in the air. Bella had almost stopped her dad from cutting the cake, because she loved looking at it so much!

After cake, the girls had watched a movie, but Bella hadn't been able to concentrate. She was too busy thinking about the waiting unicorns.

"I think it's time for presents!" Queen Katherine said.

"Yaaay!" Bella cheered. Now it was just Bella, her parents, and Ivy and Clara.

The first-floor living room overflowed with presents from Bella's family. The people of Crystal had come to the castle gates after the parade, leaving hundreds of flowers, small gifts, and cards for Bella. Bella had burst into giggles when one of the royal security guards had told her that someone had left a hen with a note explaining how fresh eggs would make Bella a healthy princess.

"This box is taller than me!" Bella exclaimed. She stood next to a box wrapped in dark-blue paper with glittery white stars. The bow on the box was the size of her head.

"That's from Grandma Margie," said Queen Katherine.

"Grandma M sends the best presents," Bella said. She smiled, thinking of her dad's mom. "I can't wait to open it."

Her eyes were trained on the presents that Clara and Ivy held. Her besties, still in their parade gowns, grinned.

"Can I open your presents first?" Bella asked her friends. Then she glanced at her mom. "In my room?"

Ivy and Clara looked to Queen Katherine for a yes or no.

"That's entirely up to Ivy and Clara," Queen Katherine said. "Perhaps they want to make you

wait, Bella, until the end of the evening." There
was a teasing tone in the queen's voice.

"Hmmm . . . maybe we should make you wait,"
Ivy said.

"Yeah, we could make you wait until you open all of your gifts," Clara said. "I'm sure you have *no* interest in opening our presents right now. . . ."

"Oh, *please*? You can't say no to the birthday girl," Bella said. "I'll be sad forever."

Queen Katherine, Ivy, and Clara laughed.

"Well, if you're going to be sad *forever,* then maybe we should let you open our gifts," Ivy said with a look at Clara.

Clara nodded. "If you'd only be sad for a day, okay, but not *forever*!"

"Yay! Let's go!" Bella cheered, dancing in the direction of her room. Ivy and Clara were right behind her.

The girls ran to Bella's room, kicked off their shoes, and hopped onto Bella's enormous bed.

"You can go first," Clara said to Ivy.

Smiling, Ivy handed a small box to Bella. It had

been wrapped with paper that kept changing from pink to purple, and there was a card attached to a curly purple bow.

Bella opened the card and read it aloud. "'Princess Bella, happy birthday! I'm so lucky to have you as my best friend! I hope this is the best day ever! Love, Ivy.'" Bella smiled at her friend. "Thank you so much. I'm lucky to have you!"

Bella ripped open the wrapping paper and found a silver photo frame dotted with colored gems. Inside was a photo of Ivy, Clara, and Bella with their arms slung across each other's shoulders as they grinned at the camera. The gems in the frame changed from red to blue to green in no particular order.

"Oh!" Bella said happily. "I love this picture! I remember when your mom took it, Ivy, when we had a sleepover at your house a few months ago. The frame is so perfect! Thank you!"

She hugged Ivy and got up to place the framed photo on her dresser.

"My turn!" Clara handed Bella a long, rectangular box. The white box was closed with a turquoise ribbon, and like Ivy's, there was a card taped to the top.

Bella took the pink envelope, opened the card covered with adorable unicorns, and smiled.

"'Hail Princess Bella! Don't get used to me calling you 'princess,' okay? Only on your BIRTHDAY! You're an amazing best friend, and I'm so happy this day is finally here! Xoxo, Clara.'"

"So you're really not going to call me 'princess' after this huge birthday?" Bella teased.

"No!" Ivy and Clara said at the same time. All of the girls burst into giggles.

Bella slid off the ribbon and lifted the box lid. She removed a sunshine-yellow cloth binder with a clear pocket in the front. She opened it and found pages of clear pockets, thick papers with color and different designs like swirls or rainbows, and some with words in glittery letters, like *SMILE!*, *BFFs*, and *SLEEPOVER*. The stickers flashed on and off so the words disappeared for a second before reappearing in a different color. The borders around the empty frames blinked and shone brightly.

"Oohhhhh! A friendship scrapbook!" Bella said. "This is perfect for all of us! We can fill the pages with pictures and pass it around."

Bella hugged Clara, who had a huge smile on her face. "I'm so happy you like it, Bells!" Clara said. "I thought it would be fun for us to keep memories in here."

Ivy climbed off the bed and searched through the CRYSTAL GIRL canvas bag that she carried everywhere. "Aha!" she said, holding up her camera.

"There's no better night to start filling the scrapbook! Say cheese!"

Bella and Clara said the magic word and grinned into the camera. Ivy left the camera floating in the air and scrambled to join them. The camera clicked and flashed.

"Print it!" Bella said.

Ivy plucked the camera out of the air and pressed a button. The photo appeared on Bella's bed.

Bella picked up the picture and slid it into the scrapbook. The photo, on repeat, captured the girls a few seconds before and after the photo was taken. Again Bella, Ivy, and Clara readied themselves for the camera, posed, and then giggled.

SLAM!

Though her mom was too far away for Bella to hear what she was saying, she heard Queen Katherine yelling downstairs. The voices of at least four or five royal security guards echoed up to Bella's room.

"What was that?" Clara and Ivy asked, looking scared.

"Stay here, okay? I'll be right back," Bella said nervously. She was off the bed and out the door before her friends could answer her. An uneasy feeling swirled in her stomach. Bella ran down a spiral staircase, through a long corridor, and skidded to a halt in the foyer.

"My Princess Bella, happy birthday, darling."

9

Queen of Mean

Bella stared at the strange woman who stood in the entrance to the castle. She had black hair cascading down her back, and the ends were bright red. Red lipstick stained the woman's mouth—one that smiled at Bella. But the smile wasn't real. Bella could see it in her eyes. They were black and without a trace of feeling.

At that moment Bella took in the guards surrounding the woman, swords drawn. In the middle of the circle, Queen Katherine stood next to her with a furious expression.

"Bella, go back upstairs," the queen said, her voice low.

The scary woman laughed. "Sister, you haven't changed at all in the years since we last gathered."

Sister?!

Bella took a closer look and realized that the strange woman looked exactly like her mom. Except a lot meaner. And with darker hair.

If this crazy woman was Queen Katherine's sister, that also meant she was Bella's . . . aunt?

Queen Katherine's head whipped away from Bella as she faced the woman.

"Speechless, Katherine? This whole"—the woman waved a pale hand at the guards—"mess could have been avoided had you sent me an invitation to Bella's eighth birthday. Silly of you and Phillip to think royal guards would keep me from my niece."

Bella's eyes widened when the woman said "niece."

"Did you see my birthday message to you, Bella?"

Bella frowned. *Birthday message?* "You?" she whispered. "You sent the red smoke?" She shook her head. "That would mean . . . you live in the Dark Forest."

The woman laughed. "More like I rule the Dark Forest, darling. I am Queen Fire, after all."

Queen Fire? Bella stared at her mom, but Queen Katherine's eyes were on her sister. Bella clenched her teeth. A cold feeling trickled down her back, and she wanted to scream at the guards to make Queen Fire leave. If this . . . relative . . . ruled the Dark Forest, she was dangerous. *Mom told me to go already,* Bella thought. *But I can't.* Her legs felt rooted to the ground.

"Darling girl, come give your aunt a hug,"

Queen Fire said, her black eyes trained on Bella. "I haven't had a glimpse of you since your birth."

"Mom?" Bella asked. "What is she talking about?"

Queen Fire's expression darkened. "You know nothing about me?"

Bella shook her head.

"We breathed not a word about you to Bella, Fawn," Queen Katherine said. "Bella didn't need to know of your existence."

Bella's mother turned to look at Bella. "Go upstairs now!" Queen Katherine's voice was sharp.

Bella hated to disobey her mother, but she wasn't going to leave her alone with guards and her apparently evil sister. *Dad, where are you?* Bella thought.

Queen Fire smiled and clasped her hands. "You were afraid, Katherine. Afraid that Bella might be like me. She certainly has my feisty spirit."

"I don't know you at all," Bella said, her heart pounding. "But if my parents kept you from me, they had a good reason. My mom doesn't want you here. And neither do I."

Queen Katherine shot Bella a look, but this time it was one of pride. Bella knew she would be grounded later for staying against her mother's wishes, but she wasn't going to let anyone upset her mom. Queen Katherine slipped away from her sister, through the circle of guards, and took Bella's side. Bella felt an instant rush of relief that her mom wasn't between the guards and Queen Fire.

Queen Fire took a step toward Bella, her long black dress skimming the floor. The royal guards jumped closer, their swords shining in the light as they pointed at the queen.

"You're young, my girl," Queen Fire said, almost in a trancelike tone. "Tell me you haven't worried about tonight."

Bella's mouth opened and closed. Suddenly she wished she'd listened to her mom and had left the room. Queen Fire was *right*—Bella had worried about the Pairing Ceremony, but why would Queen Fire expect her to have worried?

"I have my answer," Queen Fire said, a smile curling on her lips. "Bella, do you wish for something different from the life planned for you?"

"That's enough!" Queen Katherine exclaimed. "You will leave at once or—"

"Or what, Katherine?" Queen Fire asked.

"Or I will have you thrown into prison for trespassing!" King Phillip ran into the room, his sword at his side. His boots thundered on the marble floor. "Remove her immediately," he barked to the guards. "Make sure she never crosses the castle bridge again."

Bella swallowed. She'd never seen her dad so angry. The guards sprang into action, two of them taking Queen Fire by the upper arms.

"Fawn, if you *ever* set foot onto my property or speak to my wife or daughter, remember that you have been warned," King Phillip threatened.

The way Queen Fire looked at the royal family made Bella shiver.

"Don't worry about me, Phillip," Queen Fire said. "Your concern should be if and when Bella crosses the river and seeks *my* help."

"Out!" King Phillip bellowed.

"I'll see myself out," Queen Fire added. She opened her hands, palms to the sky, and the air crackled and a red cloud of smoke covered her. The guards coughed and scrambled in the smoke. But Queen Fire was gone.

"Bella." Queen Katherine placed a hand on her daughter's arm. "Are you all right?"

Bella took a few deep breaths before she looked up at her mom. "Yes. I'm sorry that I didn't go to my room. I know there were guards to protect you, but I don't trust her and—"

Queen Katherine knelt down in front of Bella. "I understand why you stayed. Thank you for wanting to protect me. I'm more concerned about you. I didn't want you to learn of Queen Fire this way."

"Is she really your sister?" Bella asked.

Queen Katherine nodded. "Bella, I'll answer all of your questions. I promise. But you have guests. Would you like to talk after Ivy and Clara have gone?"

Bella nodded, still shaking from the whole thing.

"Go upstairs and talk to Ivy and Clara," Queen Katherine said. She kissed Bella's cheek, and Bella hurried upstairs.

She reached her room and found her friends sitting wide-eyed on her bed.

"Everything is okay," Bella said immediately.

The three best friends hugged, then huddled together while Bella told them what had happened downstairs. When she reached the end of the story, Bella didn't even want to think of the words *Queen Fire* until she talked to her parents. It was too much, too fast.

10

Moonbow + Pairing Time = Good Luck?

The night air was warm, but Bella shivered. She sat on one of the stone benches outside between Queen Katherine and King Phillip. It was time to talk about Queen Fire before they made their way to the royal stables. Moments ago Bella had said good-bye to Ivy and Clara. Usually the girls would sleep over, but not tonight. Not with the Pairing Ceremony ahead. Both girls had hugged Bella tight and made her promise to call them first thing in the morning to give them all the details about her new unicorn. Thanks to Queen Fire's interruption, Bella hadn't had time to open her other gifts yet.

Bella looked up at the night sky. It twinkled with lights of thousands of stars. The moon, full and round, had given light to a rare moonbow. Usually moonbows were a symbol of good luck. Bella blinked up at the arch of colors that spread from the moon and lit up the sky. *I hope my aura is any of the moonbow colors except red,* she thought.

Her throat was tight. The visit from Queen Fire had rattled her, even though the rest of the evening had been perfect.

"I knew a bad queen lived in the Blacklands and ruled the Dark Forest, but I've never heard the name 'Queen Fire.' Until tonight," Bella began.

Suddenly the questions came to her mind rapid-fire.

"Mom, what happened to her? Why is she evil? Why didn't you and Dad tell me? Is she dangerous?" The questions tumbled out of Bella's mouth.

Queen Katherine took a deep breath. "Bella, this was not something your father and I intended to keep from you forever. We knew you would eventually learn about Queen Fire from a classmate or research. Your father and I always wanted the truth to come from us."

King Phillip nodded. "Queen Fire—Fawn—is your mother's fraternal twin sister. We do not speak of her because, yes, she is evil and she does have a grudge against our family."

"Why?" Bella asked.

"On our eighth birthday," Queen Katherine started, "Fawn and I were best friends. As close as sisters could be. We were both excited for our Pairing Ceremony that night, and I went first. My aura, as you know, turned green and I was gifted with Kiwi."

Pain flicked across the queen's face. "My sister's aura turned red. The first royal in history to have that color aura. It was something my parents had only read about in Crystal lore as a color of evil and darkness."

"Oh no," Bella whispered. "Did Queen Fire find a red unicorn that night?"

"No." Queen Katherine shook her head. "Red auras in unicorns do not naturally exist. My sister also became the first royal not to be Paired. She changed that day. The fun, caring sister I'd grown up with was gone. In her place was someone angry and jealous."

"I'm sorry, Mom," Bella said softly.

Queen Katherine lifted her head, looking out across the castle grounds at the fireflies that sparkled in the night. "At fourteen, my sister left the castle and never came back. I reached out to her, but she didn't want anything to do with me."

"Queen Fire," King Phillip said, squeezing the queen's hand, "began stealing royal unicorns—the special, highly trained ones that aren't Paired with a royal—and built a castle in the Dark Forest."

"What happens to the unicorns?" Bella asked.

"My sister's aura, which has now shifted to black, poisons the unicorns' minds," the queen explained. "They become angry, dangerous creatures. I think Fawn continues to steal unicorns because she never got one as a child."

Bella didn't know what to say. Red auras. Black auras. An evil queen who was her aunt.

Horror struck deep in Bella's stomach.

"Mom, Dad," she said. "What if . . . what if my aura is red?"

"No!" the king and queen immediately chorused.

"No, Bella," Queen Katherine repeated firmly. "That will not happen. My sister must have had something dark within her long before her Pairing Ceremony. You are my daughter—you are one of the most compassionate girls I've ever known, and I am sure you will not reveal a red aura."

King Phillip put a hand on Bella's knee. "Your mother is right. Fawn was a troubled girl who hid it very well from her sister and parents. You're nothing like that, Bella."

"My sister has nothing to lose, so she came here tonight to cause worry and doubt in your mind," Queen Katherine added. "Her own eighth birthday was so unhappy that she wants to make yours that way as well. Don't let her get to you."

Almost as if on cue, a unicorn whinnied from the stables.

Bella took a deep breath, nodding, and tried to believe her parents. She crossed all her fingers that a red aura wouldn't appear when she began the Pairing Ceremony. She didn't know what she would do if—

"Are you ready, sweetie?"

King Phillip's voice cut through Bella's thoughts. She hadn't even noticed that he and her mom had risen and were standing in front of her.

Bella nodded, slipping a sweaty hand into her dad's free cool hand. In the other, he carried a book—a very *old*-looking book.

The family approached the royal stables. It was one of Bella's favorite places on the castle grounds. Floodlights lit the stable yard and the stable entrance. The pastel-green paint on the stable's outside reminded of Bella of mint chocolate chip ice cream because of the black stable roof. All of the unicorns had been tucked away in their stalls for the night.

"Greetings, King Phillip, Queen Katherine," Frederick, the stable manager, said. "And happiest of birthdays to you, Princess Bella."

Bella's smile was wobbly. "Thank you," she said to the tall, brown-haired man.

"Follow me, please," Frederick said.

Frederick led Bella and her parents to a large arena inside the stable. The glass windows, usually where Bella loved to watch the unicorns' training, had been sprayed a frosty white. Bella couldn't see inside.

"The glass is frosted for your privacy during the ceremony," Frederick explained, as if he had read Bella's thoughts.

Frederick opened a door, bowing his head and waving for the royal family to enter ahead of him.

"You first, honey," King Phillip said. He released Bella's hand. Bella didn't realize how hard she'd been squeezing it!

She took a giant breath and walked across the dirt-covered floor. Ten gorgeous white unicorns stood in a line in front of her, each one held by a stable groom. The unicorns almost shimmered. Their manes and tails looked like silk and had a slight curl at the ends. A horn poked from under each unicorn's forelock—the mane across the unicorn's forehead. The horns weren't very long, since these were young unicorns. But each horn had a *very* pointed tip. A line etched into the horn swirled from the base to the top.

Frederick, Queen Katherine, and King Phillip formed a line next to Bella.

"Bella," Frederick said.

Bella tore her eyes away from the unicorns. "Yes?" she asked, looking past her mom.

"As the royal tradition goes, you are to start at the beginning of the unicorn line and make your way to the end. You will only need to pause for a second or two in front of each unicorn before the unicorn's aura color is revealed."

"My aura hasn't shown," Bella said, biting her bottom lip. "When will it?"

Frederick and Bella's parents smiled.

"Don't worry, Bella." King Phillip smiled. "Your aura will appear after I read a short passage from Crystal's *Royal Book*. Then you will approach the unicorns."

"Bella, please stand before your father and me," Queen Katherine said.

Bella clasped her hands together and tried to stop her knees from shaking. She moved in front of her parents, and Frederick stood off to the side.

King Phillip carefully opened the dark-brown book with the royal family crest on the front. He stopped on a page bordered in gold and looked up at Bella. Queen Katherine put an arm through one of King Phillip's arms and gave her daughter a reassuring smile. "You're ready," the queen mouthed.

My stomach doesn't feel ready! Bella thought. Her heart sounded like it was in her ears.

"Princess Isabella," King Phillip said formally.

He spoke with his this-is-very-important voice, like he had used during the parade.

"On April thirteenth," King Phillip continued, "this day in the Crystal Kingdom, you have reached the age of eight. With this birthday comes immense responsibility. You, as your royal ancestors before you, are about to participate in your Unicorn Pairing Ceremony."

Bella felt as though her dad was speaking another language for a moment. Or talking about someone else. *I can't believe this is my ceremony*, she thought.

"As the only princess of Crystal," King Phillip said, "you must acknowledge that you are in a place of great power and responsibility. Your kingdom looks up to you as its princess. If you feel that you are too young for anyone to look up to, this is untrue. Your actions will be watched with closer scrutiny by your kingdom. Your mother and I expect you to remember this and to be a kind, compassionate, relatable royal. Are you able to fulfill these duties, Princess Bella?"

"Yes, Father," Bella answered. It didn't seem like the time to say "Dad."

King Phillip smiled. "Wonderful. It is with great pleasure that your mother and I bestow upon you a chance to find a unicorn that matches your aura. This unicorn will serve not only as your unicorn to ride but as your lifelong protector. The unicorn Paired to you, Princess Bella, will be attuned to any danger around you and will fight to ensure your safety."

King Phillip closed the book and handed it to Frederick. He took Queen Katherine's hand.

"Princess Bella," Queen Katherine said, "please bow your head and repeat after me."

Bella dipped her head. *This is really happening!* she screamed to herself. She wanted to break into a dance from nerves and excitement.

"I, Princess Bella," Queen Katherine said.

"I, Princess Bella," Bella repeated.

"Ask my aura to reveal itself," the queen said.

Bella repeated the line.

"And wish it to glow while I seek my unicorn match," Queen Katherine said.

"And wish it to glow while I seek my unicorn match," Bella said.

"Aura, please present yourself now," Queen Katherine said.

Goose bumps covered Bella's arms.

"Aura, please present yourself now," Bella said.

"Raise your head, Princess Bella," instructed Queen Katherine.

Bella lifted her head. Only seconds had passed, but it felt like hours to her. Nothing appeared.

"Mom," Bella said, panic in her voice.

Before she could say another word, Bella felt a . . . *tingle* coursing through her body. She blinked fast as a light haze appeared before her. She looked down as the mist covered her hands, arms, and the rest of her body. She could feel it— her aura was about to appear!

The shimmery white soon tinted with the palest hint of lavender and kept getting darker and darker until it stopped at a royal purple.

"Ohhh!" Bella said, gasping. "It's not red!" She didn't know if she wanted to laugh or cry. She grinned instead.

"Bella! Darling, your aura is beautiful!" Queen Katherine said. Bella saw tears in her mother's eyes.

"Honey, that color is perfect for you," King Phillip agreed.

"It's so pretty!" Bella exclaimed, waving her hands in front of her and trying to touch the mist. But her fingers swiped right through the aura. "And it's one of my favorite colors!"

"Princess Bella," Frederick said. "Congratulations on your aura. It is time for you to meet the ten awaiting unicorns."

Frederick offered Bella his arm, and she took it. He led her to the beginning of the unicorn line. The king and queen tightly clasped their hands together at their sides.

Bella's pulse pounded in her ears. *Just because your aura isn't red doesn't mean any of the unicorns will match,* she reminded herself.

"Princess?" Frederick snapped Bella back to reality.

"Yes, I'm sorry," Bella said.

"Whenever you are ready, please begin the Pairing Ceremony," Frederick said.

Bella looked at the gorgeous unicorns. The creatures, like their grooms, stared straight ahead and didn't move. Not so much as a tail swished. Bella knew how much careful selection and training this group of unicorns had gone through to be here as potential candidates.

This was it.

Bella let go of Frederick's arm and took a few first shaky steps. She reached the first unicorn and stopped in front of it. She glanced into the unicorn's liquid brown eyes. *Are you my match?* Bella thought.

A soft pink haze spread quickly over the unicorn from head to tail. Disappointment gripped Bella's stomach. *It's only your first unicorn,* she told herself. *There are nine more.*

The groom holding the pink-aura unicorn led it away from the line and out of the arena.

Bella stepped in front of the second unicorn. Green.

The third unicorn turned purple before Bella even came to a full stop in front of it.

Nerves made Bella's stomach flip-flop. She

glanced at her parents. They both nodded, encouraging her with smiles.

Bella tried to smile back, but she was too nervous. *If I don't get a unicorn even though my aura isn't red, what will happen?* she thought. *There won't be another Pairing Ceremony.*

Bella lifted her head and smoothed her dress as she stepped to the fourth unicorn. The beautiful creature blinked as a yellow haze covered its body.

The fifth unicorn turned dark blue. Bella sniffed hard, determined not to cry. *But I'm halfway through,* she thought. She forced her feet forward to the sixth unicorn, almost not stopping. *I know there won't be a match,* Bella said to herself.

Her eyes were on the seventh unicorn when she heard gasps from her parents and Frederick.

Bella looked at the unicorn beside her. The

gorgeous animal's white body had covered itself in a white mist that was turning light purple. The purple deepened just like Bella's aura. Bella's heart seemed to stop—she waited for the aura to keep darkening, but nothing happened.

The aura began to float from the hindquarters forward. Bella's mouth was open as the aura floated over the unicorn's body and disappeared into the unicorn's horn. Before Bella could blink, the last bit of the haze vanished into the horn, and it twinkled with a violet light before turning back to white. Bella's aura evaporated along with the unicorn's. A purple tint remained in the unicorn's mane and tail.

"Oh!" Bella exclaimed. She threw her arms around the unicorn's neck. The unicorn's coat was soft, and it smelled like sweet hay. "You're my match!" Bella's eyes filled with tears, and she couldn't stop hugging her unicorn.

The groom holding the unicorn bowed his head. "Congratulations, Princess Bella. This guy is incredibly lucky to have you." He handed her a leather lead line—a tool for Bella to guide her unicorn. It was attached to a matching headpiece—a halter—that ran across the unicorn's muzzle and up behind his ears. The unicorn nuzzled Bella's neck. She giggled at the warm breath on her neck and the unicorn's tickly whiskers.

Her parents rushed over and threw their arms around Bella.

"Oh, sweetie!" Queen Katherine said. She hugged Bella extra hard. "What a perfect match!"

"You've got quite a unicorn here," King Phillip said. He reached out to the unicorn, who stuck her muzzle out for a rub.

A few happy tears slid down Bella's cheeks. "I was so scared! I didn't think any of them would match me!" The unicorn nudged Bella's arm and blinked at her with warm brown eyes. It was almost as if she was saying, *Don't cry.* "You're such a good girl," Bella said.

"You'll have to think of a name," said Queen Katherine.

"I've had eight years to think," Bella said. "I already know."

She looked at the unicorn before her—all *hers*—and grinned. "Her name is Glimmer," Bella said.

"Well, Glimmer," King Phillip said happily. "Welcome to our family!"

Bella threw her arms around Glimmer's neck, never wanting to let go.

HERE'S A SNEAK PEEK AT BELLA AND
GLIMMER'S NEXT ADVENTURE:

Where's Glimmer?

"Glimmer!" Princess Bella yelled before she burst into giggles. The princess's unicorn picked up the brush from Bella's hand and held it in her mouth. The shimmery white unicorn shook her head, sending her purple-tinted mane flying. It was like she was teasing Bella. "Are you excited because it's Saturday and I have all weekend to spend with you?" Bella asked.

"She's sneaky," said Ben, a boy only a few years older than Bella. Glimmer reached out her muzzle, offering Ben the brush. He took the brush, grinning. Ben had arrived a couple of days after Bella had been Paired with Glimmer. He was the nephew of Frederick, the stable manager, and he had come from the neighboring kingdom of Foris as an apprentice of his uncle. It was up to him to teach Bella about unicorn care and riding. More important, he had been assigned to help Bella and Glimmer prepare for their upcoming Crystal Kingdom debut.

It was a beautiful, sunny day in Crystal Kingdom, the land ruled by Bella's parents, King Phillip and Queen Katherine. The air smelled like honeysuckle and roses. Ben had secured Glimmer to a post just outside the royal stables with a shimmering rainbow-colored rope that was also used to help lead her around. Bees and butterflies flitted through the air, looking like confetti. A few of the bees flashed neon yellow, almost like a flashlight being turned on and off. That meant the bees had sensed pollen in the air and were headed toward a sweet-smelling flower.

The butterflies in Crystal Kingdom were more beautiful than any others in the neighboring kingdoms. Crystal butterflies had wings lined with teensy sparkles that flashed and glittered like diamonds in the sunlight.

"Thank you for showing me how to keep Glimmer clean, Ben," Bella said, lifting her hand to shield her eyes from the sun. She eyed Glimmer—her very own unicorn—who had been a gift on her eighth birthday. A gift per royal tradition, of course. The unicorn's coat was super shiny, and her mane and tail were silky after Ben had helped Bella comb them.

"No problem, Princess Bella," Ben said.

"Ben, please," Bella said. "Just call me Bella."

"Okay, Prin—I mean, Bella." Ben smiled at her.

"Do you like taking care of the unicorns?" Bella asked Ben.

Most people did not have a unicorn. It was law in Crystal Kingdom and the surrounding kingdoms that the best unicorns were saved for the royal stables. Other unicorns ran free, and it was against the law for a commoner to capture one.

Ben laughed, looking at Bella. "I love it," he said. "Uncle Frederick has taught me so much already. I don't know much about the royal customs, but I do know about unicorns."

"Did you know someone royal in Foris?" Bella asked.

"My father worked in the royal stables at Foris Castle," Ben explained. "He had been training me so I could work in the stables someday too. But he broke his arm a few weeks ago working with a royal unicorn."

Bella's long brown hair swirled around her shoulders as she whipped her head around to look at Ben.

"Ouch! I'm so sorry! Is your dad going to be okay?" she asked.

Ben nodded. "He'll be back in the stables in a couple of months, but he didn't want me to lose any time. Uncle Frederick has been training and caring for unicorns even longer than my dad, so I'll be living with him until my apprenticeship is done."

Bella climbed the white fence and looked out over Crystal Castle's grounds. She loved watching unicorns frolicking in the lush pastures. But when Bella thought about the unicorns, it reminded her of her upcoming debut with Glimmer. It was going to be here so fast—this coming Wednesday morning! It was especially exciting because it was a holiday and there would be no school.

It was royal tradition that within the first month of a prince or princess being Paired with a unicorn, the pair presented themselves to the kingdom. Bella's parents had told her that the people of Crystal Kingdom were eager to see the princess and her unicorn.

Bella couldn't wait to introduce Glimmer to the townspeople!

Bella shifted her gaze back to Glimmer as Ben climbed the fence to sit next to her. She'd only been Paired with Glimmer a week ago, but she loved her unicorn more than anything in the entire Crystal Kingdom (well, except her parents!). Definitely more than all of the people in the other three sky islands. Bella had learned in geography class that sky islands were pieces of land that floated high in the clouds. The only way to reach another sky island was to cast a spell to create a rainbow or moonbeam to walk over as a bridge between two islands.

"I can't believe I got so lucky," Bella said. Glimmer pointed her cute ears in Bella's direction. "My eighth birthday was so scary!"

"How do eighth birthdays work for princes and princesses?" Ben asked.

"Well, every royal is born with an aura," Bella explained. "It's this kind of light that shows when a royal turns eight and when they are crowned king or queen. It can be any color of the rainbow." She paused, frowning. "Except for red."

"So red auras don't exist?" Ben asked.

"Actually, they *do*. But if someone's born with a red aura, it's a very, very bad sign. Have you heard of Queen Fire?"

Ben nodded quickly. "My uncle warned me about her. He told me never to enter the Dark Forest and explained that Queen Fire was, like, your family's enemy."

"Actually, Queen Fire," Bella said, taking a big gulp of air, "is my aunt. She is the first royal in history to be born with a red aura." She squeezed her eyes half-shut, peeking at Ben through her lashes. *I hope I didn't scare him by telling him a crazy evil queen is related to me,* Bella worried.

"Whoa," Ben said. "I didn't know Queen Fire was related to you. My uncle didn't tell me that part. That must have been scary for you when you waited for your aura to appear."

"It was!" Bella agreed. "My mom's is green and my dad's is yellow. Once I learned about my aunt, I got scared that my aura might be red."

Ben laughed, his brown eyes twinkling. "I haven't known you that long, but there's *no* way your aura ever could have been red."

"Thanks, Ben," Bella said. "Only my best friends, Clara and Ivy, know Queen Fire is related to me. I hope you don't want to stop teaching me now that you know."

Ben reached out a hand to stroke Glimmer's forehead. "No way. No evil queen relative is going to scare me off from helping you with Glimmer." He grinned, a mischievous glint in his eyes. "You've got a lot to learn, Princess."

Bella laughed. "Oh, really? Well, I'm glad you're sticking around then."

"Let's take Glimmer for a walk, and you can tell me more about being a royal," Ben said.

Bella nodded, and Ben untied Glimmer, handing the soft rope to Bella.

The three set off down a familiar path that wound through the castle grounds and circled one of the castle's many lakes.

"My aura appeared during the Pairing Ceremony on the night of my birthday," Bella explained.

"A Pairing Ceremony is where you're matched to your unicorn, right?" Ben asked as he walked beside Bella.

"Yes. I got this strange tingly feeling, and a purple fog surrounded me. It was my aura. Your uncle Frederick asked me to walk in front of unicorns that he had picked for me."

"He told me a little about that part," Ben said.

"Each royal unicorn glowed, showing its aura, and you had to keep going until you found one that matched you, right?"

"That's right," Bella said. She, Ben, and Glimmer continued walking through the cropped grass toward the lake. "I was getting so scared that none of the unicorns would turn purple. Then I stepped in front of Glimmer, and it was so magical. She changed from white to purple in seconds!"

"That is *so* cool! I can't wait until I'm old enough to help during a Pairing Ceremony." Ben got a faraway look in his eyes, as if he was picturing himself in Frederick's place.

"I felt this instant bond with Glimmer," Bella said. She reached up a hand and patted the unicorn's neck as they walked. "I'd been dreaming about my eighth birthday my entire life, and Glimmer has made me so happy."

Glimmer snorted and bobbed her head.

"I think she's happy too," Ben said.

Bella, Ben, and Glimmer reached the lake. A spell had been cast on the deep water so it was clear enough that the bottom of the lake was visible. Bella and Ben led Glimmer to the lake's edge and halted her. Glimmer watched Ben and Bella peer into the water, then turned her own gaze to the lake water.

"Ooh, look!" Bella said. "See those spiky blue fish?" A school of electric-blue fish covered in spikes swam near the water's edge.

"Yeah! Look over there," Ben said, pointing. "There's a huge dog fish at the bottom of the lake."

Bella's eyes followed Ben's finger. It took a moment before she spotted the dog fish. The white fish had dozens of black spots and barely moved as it crawled along the lake's bottom. It had floppy ears that covered its gills, and instead of a fish mouth it had a dog's snout. Dog fish were important to lake life—they ate all the dirty algae and helped keep the water clean. Dog fish reminded Bella of vacuum cleaners.

Glimmer pulled on the rainbow line, stretching her neck toward the lake. Ben nodded his okay, and Bella let Glimmer lower her head and take a few sips of water.

"Want to try taking Glimmer for a ride tomorrow?" Ben asked.

"Really? Do you think I'm ready?" Bella asked. She clasped her hands together and tried very hard not to jump up and down.

"Definitely!" Ben said. "I think you guys are ready."

"Yaaay!" Bella cheered. Glimmer lifted her head from the lake, and water dripped off her chin whiskers. Giggling, Bella hugged her neck. "Silly girl. We get to go riding tomorrow! Our very first ride together."

"My friends Clara and Ivy are coming over tomorrow," Bella said to Ben. "They'll be so excited to see me ride Glimmer for the first time."

The trio stayed by the lake for a few more moments before starting the walk back to the royal stables. For the rest of the day, all Bella could think about was riding. It felt like her birthday all over again!

Mermaid Tales

Exciting under-the-sea adventures
with Shelly and her mermaid friends!